TREEHOUSE TALES

Andy Griffiths lives in an amazing treehouse with his friend Terry and together they make funny books, just like the one you're holding in your hands right now. Andy writes the words and Terry draws the pictures. If you'd like to know more, read the Treehouse series (or visit www.andygriffiths.com.au).

Terry Denton lives in an amazing treehouse with his friend Andy and together they make funny books, just like the one you're holding in your hands right now. Terry draws the pictures and Andy writes the words. If you'd like to know more, read the Treehouse series (or visit www.terrydenton.com.au).

Climb higher every time
with the Treehouse series

TREEHOUSE TALES

TOO SILLY TO BE TOLD ... UNTIL NOW!

BY

ANDY GRIFFITHS

& TERRY DENTON

MACMILLAN CHILDREN'S BOOKS

First published 2022 by Pan Macmillan Australia Pty Limited

First published in the UK 2023 by Macmillan Children's Books
an imprint of Pan Macmillan
The Smithson, 6 Briset Street, London EC1M 5NR
EU representative: Macmillan Publishers Ireland Ltd, 1st Floor,
The Liffey Trust Centre, 117–126 Sheriff Street Upper
Dublin 1, D01 YC43
Associated companies throughout the world
www.panmacmillan.com

ISBN 978-1-5290-8867-0

Text copyright © Backyard Stories 2022
Illustrations copyright © Terry Denton 2022

The right of Andy Griffiths and Terry Denton to be identified as the
author and illustrator of this work has been asserted by them in
accordance with the Copyright, Designs and Patents Act 1988.

3 5 7 9 8 6 4 2

A CIP catalogue record for this book is available from the British Library.

Typeset in 13 /18 FreightText Pro by Seymour Designs
Printed and bound by CPI Group (UK) Ltd, Croydon CR0 4YY

CONTENTS

The Magic Wand

'Hey, Andy,' said Terry one day when we were out walking in the forest. 'Look at this cool stick I found—it's got a little star on the end!'

'That's not a stick,' I said. 'That's a **magic wand**! You should be careful with it. Whatever you do, don't point it at anyone and say, "Abracadabra".'

'Why not?' said Terry.

'Because it's magic!' I said. '*Anything* could happen.'

'Okay,' said Terry. 'I'll be careful.'

'Promise?' I said.

'Yes,' said Terry.

'Good,' I said.

'Hey, Andy!' said Terry, pointing the magic wand at me.

'Abracadabra!'

Suddenly I felt very **strange**.

The next thing I knew I had four legs, a tail and was covered in fur. Just like a dog.

And that's because I *was* a dog!

'Now look what you've done!' I said. (Although it didn't come out like that. It just came out as, 'BARK! BARK! BARK!')

That's when Jill came along. 'Oh, what a nice little doggy,' she said, patting me on the head. 'What's his name?'

'Andy,' said Terry.

'*Andy*?' said Jill.

'Yes,' said Terry. 'I accidentally turned Andy into a dog with this magic wand I found.'

'Are you going to turn him back?' said Jill.

'I'm not sure,' said Terry. 'I've always wanted a dog.'

'And he *is* a cute dog,' said Jill, patting me on the head again.

'Yes,' said Terry. 'Actually, I think I like him better this way. Don't you?'

Jill nodded slowly. 'Yeah, I think I do,' she said, ruffling my ears.

I was about to get mad but then I realised I couldn't get mad because I was happy. I *loved* being a dog. I loved my fur coat. And I loved having a tail—it was so much fun to wag. I wagged it and wagged it and wagged it.

Terry and Jill both patted me and told me I was a good boy. I rolled over and they scratched my stomach. It felt nice.

'Here, boy,' said Terry. 'Let's play fetch.' And then he threw the magic wand into the forest.

I couldn't help what happened next. I just *had* to chase that magic wand. Thanks to my two extra legs I found I could run faster than I'd ever run before. I could smell every single smell there was to smell . . . including the *magic wand* smell, which led me straight to the magic wand. I picked it up with my mouth, ran back to Terry and Jill and dropped it at their feet. Jill picked it up and threw it again, and I chased it down and brought it back.

Jill and Terry took turns throwing
the wand and every time they threw
it I ran after it, until one time,
after Terry threw it, I couldn't find it.

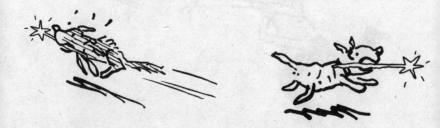

I sniffed and sniffed, searching for it until I finally found it, but it was lying next to something that smelled even better.

Mud!

A big, muddy mud puddle, which I threw myself into. I rolled around on my back with my legs in the air like I just didn't care . . . and that's because I didn't. I was too happy to care about anything!

(I don't know if you've ever rolled around in a big, muddy mud puddle, but if you haven't, I recommend doing it as soon as you possibly can.)

I rolled around for quite a long time—so long that Terry and Jill came over to see why I hadn't brought the magic wand back.

'Andy!' said Terry. 'Get out of that puddle!'

I got out and began to shake the mud off my fur.

Jill and Terry jumped back.

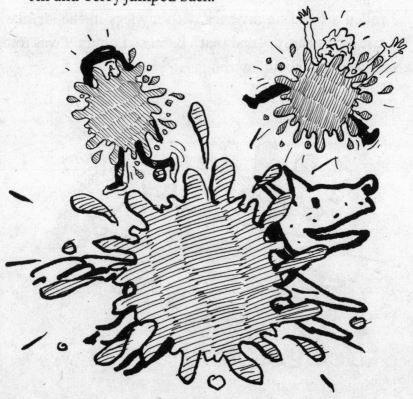

'Stop it, Andy!' said Terry. 'You're getting mud all over us!'

The thing is, though, when you're a dog and you start shaking it's hard to stop.

So even though I *wanted* to stop I *couldn't* stop and the more I tried *not* to shake the more I shook.

'QUIT IT, ANDY!' said Terry, who was now as muddy as I was before I started shaking.

'I don't think he can help it,' said Jill, who was almost as muddy as Terry.

'Well, I'll turn him into something else then!' said Terry.

He reached down, picked up the magic wand and pointed it at me.

But before he could say the magic word I leapt through the air, grabbed it with my teeth and started to run away.

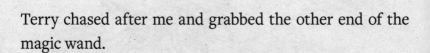

Terry chased after me and grabbed the other end of the magic wand.

'Let go, Andy!' he said. 'We're not playing tug of war!'

Yes, we are! I thought. This was fun! I pulled and pulled and Terry pulled and pulled, but he was stronger than me and he pulled the magic wand out of my mouth so hard that he fell backwards and ended up sprawled on the ground.

I leapt on top of him, trying to get the magic wand back. I'm not sure exactly what happened next but at some point Terry yelled,

'Abracadabra!'

What Terry didn't realise, however, was that in all the confusion he was pointing the wand at himself!

The next thing we knew Terry had four legs, a tail and was covered in fur. Just like a dog.

And that's because he *was* a dog.

An **ANGRY** dog.

'GRRRRR!' said Terry, baring his teeth at me.

There was only one thing to do.

I dropped down on my front paws and barked a

friendly LET'S PLAY! bark.

Being a dog, Terry couldn't help
but accept my invitation . . . and then
the play was **ON!**

BARK!

We chased each other around and around the mud puddle and then dived right into the middle.

'Hey, save some mud for me!' said Jill, picking up the wand, pointing it at herself and shouting,

'Abracadabra!'

The next thing we knew Jill had four legs, a tail and was covered in fur, too. Just like us!

'Bark!' she barked, throwing herself into the mud puddle as well.

We all rolled around in the mud puddle for a long time and then we all had a good long shake and chased each other around for the rest of the afternoon until we all got tired and lay down, panting, and fell asleep on the ground.

Later when we woke up we found the magic had worn off—we weren't dogs any more.

'That was fun,' I said.

'It sure was!' said Jill. 'I love dogs but I never thought I'd actually get to *be* one!'

'Woof!' said Terry.

The End

The Day We Put Chairs Up Our Noses

'Hey, Terry,' I said. 'Why do you have a chair up your nose?'

'Because it's **Chair-Up-Your-Nose Day**,' he said. 'Looks cool, doesn't it? Here, let me put a chair up *your* nose.'

'No way!' I said.

'Yes way!' said Terry, grabbing a chair and shoving it up my nose.

(I don't know if your best friend has ever shoved a chair up *your* nose, but if they have you'll know that it doesn't hurt as much as you might think. And it actually *does* look pretty cool.)

'Happy?' said Terry.

'You bet!' I said.
'So happy I feel like singing!'

'Let's sing the I've-got-a-chair-up-my-nose song!' said Terry.

'Okay,' I said. 'What are the words?'

'I don't know yet,' said Terry.
'We'll make them up as we go along. Ready, set, go!'

We each took a deep breath and started singing.

♪ Up my nose I've got a chair! ♪
Yes, that's right, there's a chair up there!
I have not in the world a care
Because up my nose I have—♫

'A chair?!' said Bill the postman, who had just arrived, carrying a large parcel.

'Yes!' I said. 'How did you guess, Bill?'

'Well, I'm no genius,' said Bill, 'but I see that each of you has a chair up your nose and it *is* Chair-Up-Your-Nose Day, so I put two and two together. I figured if anybody would have chairs up their noses on Chair-Up-Your-Nose Day it would be you and Terry.'

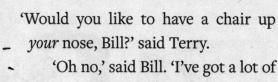

'Would you like to have a chair up *your* nose, Bill?' said Terry.

'Oh no,' said Bill. 'I've got a lot of mail to deliver. I'm much too busy to be putting chairs up my nose.'

'It doesn't take long,' I said, and before I'd even finished speaking, Terry had shoved a chair up Bill's nose.

'Oh . . . my . . .' said Bill, a little surprised. 'If I didn't know better, I'd say I had a chair up my nose!'

'You do!' I said. 'Let's sing the song!'

So we made up another verse of the song.

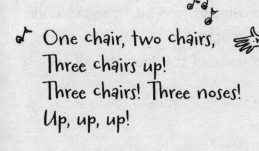

♪ One chair, two chairs,
Three chairs up!
Three chairs! Three noses!
Up, up, up!

Just as we finished singing, Jill arrived with a chair up *her* nose!

'How did you know it was Chair-Up-Your-Nose Day, Jill?' I said.

'Because I heard you singing!' said Jill. 'It sounded like fun, so I came over to join in.'

We made up *another* verse of the song and all sang it together.

♪ Three cheers for chairs! ♫
Hip hip hooray!
For chairs are jolly good nose-fillers
And so we all do say! ♫

And then the Trunkinator came in and we put a chair up his trunk and made up an extra-long verse of the song to match the Trunkinator's extra-long trunk.

♪ If you're feeling sad ♫
Or unhappy or blue,
Stick a chair up your nose
It's what you should do!
Stick a chair up your nose
Today is the day!
Stick a chair up your nose
Do it now—don't delay!

← Tamboorine

And then Edward Scooperhands, Mary Lollipoppins, Fancy Fish, Pinchy McPhee, Superfinger, Pinky and all the penguins came in, and guess what? Yep, that's right—we put chairs up their noses and sang all the verses of our song *over and over and over again*, as loudly as we could for the rest of the day and night.

'This is the *best* Chair-Up-Your-Nose Day ever!' shouted Terry.

'Having a chair up your nose is much more fun than I ever dreamed it would be,' said Jill. 'Just one question—how do you get the chairs *out* again?'

'That's a good question,' I said. 'But why would you even want to?'

'Because it's nearly midnight,' said Jill. 'Chair-Up-Your-Nose Day is almost over.'

Everybody stopped singing and playing their instruments and turned to us with worried faces.

'I need to get this chair out of my nose immediately,' said Superfinger. 'There are people out there with problems requiring finger-based solutions and I can't help them if I have a chair up my nose.'

'Me neither,' said Pinky.

'And I need to get this chair out of *my* nose and open up the ice-cream parlour,' said Edward Scooperhands.

'At midnight?' I said.

'It's never too late for ice-cream,' said Edward.

'Or lollipops,' said Mary. 'But I can't sell them with a chair up my nose. Especially if it's not Chair-Up-Your-Nose Day any more. It would just **look silly.**'

'And I need to extract this chair from my nose and get on with my mail delivery,' said Bill. 'Whoever heard of a postman with a chair up his nose? It's highly irregular. We need to remove these chairs from our noses *right now*!'

'I'm sorry,' I said, 'but I only know how to put chairs *up* noses—I have no idea how to get them out again. Do you, Terry?'

'No,' said Terry. 'We'll just have to make it Chair-Up-Your-Nose Day *every* day.'

Everybody groaned.

'Unless . . .' said Terry, thoughtfully stroking one of the chair legs sticking out of his nostril.

'Unless what?' I said.

'Unless the package Bill delivered contains what I think it does,' said Terry.

He tore the brown paper wrapping
off the parcel and opened the box.

'Yes!' he said. 'It's the **Chair-
Up-Your-Nose Extractor**
I ordered last week!'

'Three cheers for Terry,' I said.

'You mean three *chairs*!' said Jill and we all laughed
and *chaired* him enthusiastically and didn't stop
chairing until he had extracted all the chairs from our
noses. (I don't know if you've ever had a chair up your
nose, but if you have you'll probably know that the only
thing that feels better than having a chair up your nose
is the sheer relief of having it removed.)

'That was an exciting day,' I said. 'I wonder what day it will be tomorrow?'

'I hope it's Chair-Up-Your-Nose Day again,' said Terry.

'I don't think you can have the same day twice in a row,' said Jill. 'I hope it's Rhinoceros-In-Your-Ear Day tomorrow. I love rhinoceroses.'

'I like them, too,' I said. 'But I'm not sure I'd want one in my ear.'

Jill thought for a moment. 'What about up your jumper?'

'Well, that's different,' I said. 'In fact, that sounds like fun! I hope tomorrow *is* Rhinoceros-Up-Your-Jumper Day.'

'Me too,' said Terry.

The End

The Big Jump Jumping Contest

'Hey, Andy,' said Jill. 'I bet I can jump higher than you.'

'I bet you can't,' I said.

'I bet I *can*,' said Jill. 'Let's have a jumping contest and I'll prove it!'

'Any time,' I said. 'Right now, if you want.'

'Can I be in it too?' said Terry.

'Sure,' said Jill. 'But you're not going to win, because I can definitely jump higher than *both* of you.'

'And I bet I can jump higher than both of *you*,' said Terry.

'And I can jump higher than both of you *and* me!' I said.

'You can jump higher than *yourself*?' said Jill. 'How is that even possible?'

'You'll see,' I said. 'Let the big jump jumping contest begin.

Ready . . .

set . . .

GO!'

On the first jump, I jumped higher than Jill and Terry.

On the second jump, Jill jumped higher than Terry and me.

On the third jump, we all jumped as high as each other, but when Jill and I landed, Terry was nowhere to be seen.

'He must have run away to hide when he realised that we could jump so much higher than him,' I said.

'I don't think so,' said Jill. 'Look up there!'

I looked up—and there, far above us in the sky, was Terry!

He'd jumped so high he was
as high as the clouds.

'Come back, Terry!' I shouted. 'You win!'

But Terry was too far away to hear me.

And he kept going higher. And higher. And higher.

'Uh-oh,' I said. 'If he doesn't stop, he'll end up in outer space. We have to get him back.'

'But how?' Jill said. 'We'll never be able to reach him because neither of us can jump that high!'

'I've got an idea,' I said, handing Jill a pair of jet-powered jumping boots. 'Put these on. I invented them in our secret underground laboratory last week. Luckily, I made two pairs.'

Jill and I put on the jumping boots and then we jumped as high as we could.

We jumped up almost as high as the clouds, which was quite high, but nowhere near high enough.

'We need to get higher!' I said as we landed back in the treehouse—surprisingly softly thanks to the reverse-thrust feature I'd built into the jumping boots.

'I've got an idea,' said Jill.

'Let's eat some

j^umpⁱng beaⁿs.

I've got some right here.'

We each ate *three* jumping beans (which, in case you didn't know, is a *lot* of jumping beans) and jumped again.

This time—helped by the jet-powered jumping boots *and* the jumping beans—we jumped right up through the clouds . . . but it *still* wasn't high enough.

We landed back down in the forest this time.

'What are we going to do?' I said. 'Terry's still up there and we're still down here!'

Suddenly, everything went dark.

And **slimy**. And **SMELLY**.

It felt like a frogpotamus had landed on me
and swallowed my head.

  And for a good reason: because that's
exactly what had just happened.

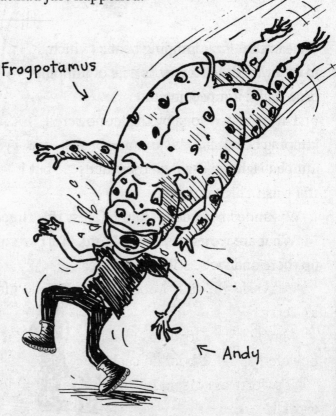

Frogpotamus

← Andy

'Sorry about that,' said Jill as she
pulled the frogpotamus off me.
'I've told it not to jump out of trees
and attach itself to people's heads
but it's very stubborn.'

'That's okay,' I said, wiping away
the slime. 'Frogpotamuses will be
frogpotamuses, I guess. But perhaps that's a *good* thing.
Maybe it could help us rescue Terry. It's pretty good at
jumping, isn't it?'

'Yes,' said Jill. 'But I don't think it could jump as high
as Terry.'

'Maybe not on its own,' I said, 'but what if we put a jet-
powered jumping boot on each of its feet?'

'It's worth a try,' said Jill. 'And I'll feed it a jumping bean
as well.'

So that's what we did.

When the frogpotamus was all jumping-booted and jumping-beaned up, we climbed onto its back.

'Ready?' said Jill.

'Yes!' I said.

'Okay,' said Jill.

She tugged gently on the frogpotamus's ear and shouted,

'JUMP!'

The frogpotamus jumped and up we went.

We went up as high as the clouds . . . and then kept on going!

We went up higher than the top of the clouds . . . and *still* kept on going!

We went up higher than the troposphere and higher than the stratosphere until we were right on the edge of space. We were almost as high up as Terry . . . and then we went even higher!

But just as I thought we were about to go
into outer space, the frogpotamus flipped
over and started falling down, back
towards Terry, opened its mouth
and swallowed Terry's head!

Then we all began falling back to Earth.

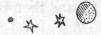

Down, down, down we fell.

Back **down** through the stratosphere,

back **down** through the troposphere,

and back **down** through the clouds,

until we landed in the treehouse.

Jill and I climbed off the frogpotamus's back, and Jill used a stick to prise its mouth open so that we could pull Terry's head out.

'I told you I could jump the highest,' said Terry, wiping handfuls of sticky slime from his face. 'I won!'

'No, you didn't,' I said. 'The frogpotamus jumped higher than you, so the frogpotamus won.'

'Actually,' said Jill, 'Andy and I were sitting on the frogpotamus's back, so technically we were even higher than the frogpotamus. That means *we* won.'

'But it wasn't a sitting-on-a-frogpotamus's-back jumping competition,' said Terry. 'And the frogpotamus wasn't even in the competition anyway. It was supposed to be a jumping competition between me, you and Andy. So, really, *I* won.'

'I think we *all* won,' I said. 'You, Jill, me *and* the frogpotamus.'

'But that's not FAIR!' shouted Terry.

'It IS fair!' I shouted back.

'IT'S NOT!'

'IT IS!'

'I CAN SHOUT LOUDER THAN YOU!' shouted Terry.

'NO, YOU CAN'T!' I shouted back. **'I CAN SHOUT LOUDER THAN YOU!'**

'I CAN SHOUT LOUDER THAN BOTH OF YOU!' shouted Jill. **'HEY, I KNOW! LET'S HAVE A BIG SHOUT SHOUTING CONTEST!'**

'GREAT IDEA!' I shouted.
'LET THE BIG
SHOUT SHOUTING
CONTEST BEGIN.

Ready . . .

set...

GO!'

The End

The Super-Duper Sucker-Upperer

'Hey, Terry,' I said. 'It's time to clean up the treehouse.'

'Why?' said Terry.

'Because it's a mess, that's why,' I said. 'It looks like a tornado came through here.'

'That's because a tornado *did* come through here,' said Terry. 'Last night. Remember? If anybody should clean up, it's that tornado!'

'Well, the tornado has gone now so I suppose it will have to be us.'

'But *we* can't do it!' said Terry.

'Why not?' I said.

'Because we only like doing fun things,' said Terry. 'And cleaning up is boring, and *boring* is not fun!'

'We can make it fun,' I said.

'How?' said Terry.

'By singing a little song as we clean,' I said. 'Like this one:

♪ Cleaning up is lovely,
  Cleaning up is fun!
  Cleaning up is exciting
  Cleaning up is—'

'DUMB!' shouted Terry. 'I've got a better idea. I'm going to the secret underground laboratory to invent a cleaning machine to do all the cleaning for us.'

'I'm not sure that's such a good idea,' I said.

But he had already gone.

Not for long, though.

'I've done it!'

he said when he came back. 'I've invented the

world's most amazing
cleaning machine!'

'Well, where is it?' I said. 'I can't see any amazing cleaning machine.'

'It's right here,' said Terry, holding out his hand to reveal a small box. 'Ta da! Behold the **SUPER-DUPER SUCKER-UPPERER!** It can suck up every piece of dirt, dust and mud in the entire treehouse. It can also suck up banana skins, breadcrumbs, dirty underwear, smelly socks,

COOL!

leaves, paper, cardboard, dead bugs, marshmallow molecules, popcorn kernels, chocolate stains, ice-cream drips, pizza droppings and lollipop sticks.'

'What about pens with no ink, blunt pencils, bird feathers, flying cat fur and dinosaur scales?' I said.

'Yes, yes, yes, yes and yes!' said Terry. 'The **SUPER-DUPER SUCKER-UPPERER** can suck up *all* of those things, and anything else that comes under the category of rubbish.'

'Well, what are we waiting for?' I said. 'Turn it on!'

'Okay,' said Terry. He put the **SUPER-DUPER SUCKER-UPPERER** on the ground. 'Stand back and prepare to be amazed!'

Terry squeezed the small box and it began to buzz. Then it began to shake. It buzzed and shook and made a noise that sounded like a vacuum cleaner, except it was much, much louder.

And then a long, wavy tube shot out of it and began to suck.

It sucked.

And sucked.

The **SUPER-DUPER SUCKER-UPPERER** sucked up all the dust, dirt and mud from the floor around it.

Then it sucked up the scraps of food, bits of paper and all the other rubbish in the room. It was incredible. Within moments the entire room was clean and clutter-free. I was starting to think this might be the best thing Terry had ever invented when, without warning, it sucked up a chair.

And then another chair.

And then *all* the chairs.

'Hey!' I said. 'The chairs aren't rubbish!'

'What?' said Terry. 'I can't hear you—the **SUPER-DUPER SUCKER-UPPERER** is making a lot of noise sucking up all the chairs!'

'I SAID, THE CHAIRS AREN'T RUBBISH!'

'Good point,' said Terry. 'I think it needs a little adjusting.'

He pulled a screwdriver out of his pocket and kneeled in front of the **SUPER-DUPER SUCKER-UPPERER**. But before he could make any adjustments, the tiny machine sucked the screwdriver right out of his hand.

'Hey!' he said. And that was the last thing he said before the **SUPER-DUPER SUCKER-UPPERER** sucked in his hand . . . and then his arm . . . and then the rest of him as well!

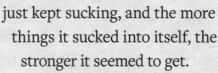

'Uh-oh,' I said, backing away. The **SUPER-DUPER SUCKER-UPPERER** just kept sucking, and the more things it sucked into itself, the stronger it seemed to get.

Aside from the chairs and the screwdriver and Terry, it sucked up the marshmallow machine, the vegetable vaporiser and a whole bunch of penguins.

save me!

None of these things were rubbish, either. (Well, except maybe for Terry—I can see how the **SUPER-DUPER SUCKER-UPPERER** might have got confused in his case.)

I ran from the room before it could suck me up as well. It followed me, sucking up everything in its path!

It sucked up Mary Lollipoppins and all of her lollipops.

It sucked up Edward Scooperhands, all his ice-cream cones and every one of his 78 tubs of ice-cream.

It sucked up the automatic tattoo machine, the Maze of Doom and more penguins. The Trunkinator put up a brave fight. He tried to punch the **SUPER-DUPER SUCKER-UPPERER**, but its sucking power was stronger than his punching power, and it sucked him up as well.

It wasn't long before the **SUPER-DUPER SUCKER-UPPERER** had sucked up every level of the treehouse, every branch of the tree, the trunk of the tree, every other tree in the forest, Jill's house, and Jill and all her animals.

There was just me left.

And then it sucked up me as well!

Everything went black.

I found myself flying around in a whirling, swirling world of dust and mud and dirt and animals and stuff—*so much stuff!* And just when I thought I couldn't take it any more, I had to take it some more. And just when I thought I couldn't take that any more either, I had to take even *that* some more . . . And then there was a massive explosion and everything—including me—went flying out of the **SUPER-DUPER SUCKER-UPPERER** into every nook, cranny and corner of the treehouse.

It was the *biggest mess* I'd ever seen, even bigger than the mess caused by the tornado.

The contents of the treehouse were all mixed up with the forest and the animals and all the stuff the **SUPER-DUPER SUCKER-UPPERER** had sucked up.

'What happened?' said Jill, who was hanging from the branch of a nearby tree.

'Terry made a **SUPER-DUPER SUCKER-UPPERER** to help us clean up the treehouse,' I said. 'But it sucked up *everything*—including us. And then it exploded! And now the treehouse is even messier than it was before!'

'Well, I guess we'll just have to clean it up again,' said Jill.

'But cleaning up is boring!' said Terry, who was covered in so much rubbish it was hard to tell where the rubbish stopped and Terry started.

'Not for my animals it isn't,' said Jill. 'They love cleaning up and they're really good at it!

Come on, gang— get cleaning!'

floor

Jill was right.

Her animals *were* really good at cleaning.

Her horses dusted with their tails, Manny the goat ate all the rubbish, Pink the camel spat cleaning fluid everywhere (it turns out camel humps are full of cleaning fluid—who knew?!) and all of her rabbits followed behind polishing all the surfaces with their soft fluffy tails. Meanwhile, Silky and the other flying cats flew around the branches removing debris and licking the leaves clean. (The other animals, including the treehouse animals, did what they could, which wasn't much, but it was better than nothing, although not *that* much better.)

Pretty soon the treehouse was spick and span—in fact, it was spicker and spanner than it had been before the tornado.

And so we celebrated with a huge popcorn and marshmallow feast, followed by the world's biggest bun and refrigerator fight. Sure, things got a bit messy, but the animals cleaned it all up again . . . and again . . . and again . . .

The End

The Return of Professor Stupido

'Hey, Andy,' said Terry, 'don't look now but there's a huge spider up there!'

Of course I looked, then immediately wished I'd taken Terry's advice and *not* looked, because I saw the biggest, ugliest, hairiest spider I'd ever seen.

'Ugh!' I said. 'I wish spiders had never been invented. Where's Professor Stupido when you need him?'

'I'm right here!'

said a familiar voice.

'PROFESSOR STUPIDO

THE GREATEST UN·INVENTOR IN THE WORLD, AT YOUR SERVICE!'

We turned to see a ridiculous-looking man wearing striped pants, a checked jacket and a small black bow tie: a man I had hoped *never* to see again.

(You've heard of inventors who invent things? Well, Professor Stupido is an *un*-inventor, with the power to *un*-invent things simply by pointing at them and saying a little rhyme.)

'Professor Stupido?!' I said. 'But that's impossible! We tricked you into un-inventing yourself!'

'Yes, that's correct,' he said. 'You did. And a pretty good trick it was, too. But I am such a brilliant un-inventor that I was able to un-invent my own un-invention!'

'That doesn't make any sense,' said Terry. 'How could you un-invent your own un-invention if you no longer existed to un-invent it?'

'I admit I don't fully understand it myself,' said Professor Stupido. 'And yet, here I am—at your service. Now, what would you like me to un-invent for you?'

'Well, since you're here, we'd like you to un-invent spiders, please,' said Terry.

'With pleasure,' said Professor Stupido, focusing his intense gaze on the spider.

'You are creepy and crawly
And venomous, too
It will be my great pleasure
To un-invent you!'

He raised his hand to point at the spider,
but before he could transmit his deadly
un-inventing power I pushed his hand down.

'Wait!' I said.

'What did you do that for?' said Professor Stupido,
annoyed. 'I was just about to make the world a safer and
much more pleasant place by un-inventing spiders!'

'*Maybe* the world would be a better place without
spiders,' I said. 'But then again, maybe it wouldn't.'

'How could a world in which spiders exist be better
than a world in which they don't?' said Professor Stupido.

'Yeah,' said Terry. 'Explain *that*, Andy!'

'Well,' I said, 'I don't like spiders any more than
you do, but they do perform an important
service by eating bugs like mosquitoes and
flies. If spiders weren't around to eat the
bugs, then the treehouse—
and the world—might be a
much more *un*pleasant place.'

'That's a good point,' said Terry.

'Yes,' said Professor Stupido. 'But I have a much better solution: I'll not only un-invent spiders; I'll un-invent bugs as well! Stand back!'

'You sting and nip and whine
And bite and buzz and linger
I hereby un-invent spiders and bugs
With the power of my finger!'

ARGH!

He raised his hand again to point at the spider—and presumably any bugs unlucky enough to be in the area—but once again I pushed his arm down.

'Wait!' I said.

'Why?!' said Professor Stupido. 'I was just about to make the world a much less annoying place by un-inventing spiders *and* bugs.'

'Maybe the world would be a less annoying place without spiders and bugs,' I said. 'But then again, maybe it wouldn't. Birds eat a *lot* of spiders and bugs. If you took spiders and bugs away, birds might not have anything to eat. A world without birds would be *much* more unpleasant than a world *with* them.'

'That's a good point,' said Terry. 'I didn't think about that. I love looking at birds and all their beautiful shapes and colours—and I love listening to them as well. I'd really miss them if they weren't here.'

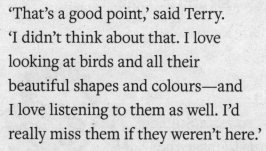

'Never fear,' said Professor Stupido. 'I'll not only un-invent spiders, bugs *and* birds, I'll un-invent everybody's eyes and ears so that nobody will miss anything! It will be the best of all possible worlds!'

'Birds and eyes and flapping ears
We've had enough of you.
Consider yourself un-invented
Thanks for your service—now you're through!'

Professor Stupido raised his hand for a third time—and for a third time, I pushed his arm back down.

'Wait!' I said.

'What now?' said Professor Stupido impatiently. 'I'm trying to make the world a better place and all you do is keep interrupting me!'

'Sorry,' I said, 'but I'm not sure the world *would* be a better place without eyes and ears, even if there were no birds to see or hear. Besides, I kind of like my eyes and ears.'

'Me too,' said Terry. 'Without eyes, nobody would be able to see *anything*. And without ears, nobody would be able to hear anything, either.'

'Those are both excellent points, Terry,' I said.

'No, they're not,' said Professor Stupido. 'I have a much better solution. I'll un-invent all sights and sounds as well. Then there'll be nothing to see or hear in the first place. And while I'm at it, I'll un-invent smells, taste and touch. Actually, come to think of it, I might as well un-invent the entire universe again.'

'Oh no you won't,' said Terry.

'Oh yeah?' said Professor Stupido. 'And how do you propose to stop me?'

'Like this!' said Terry, raising his arm and pointing his finger directly at Professor Stupido.

'Professor Stupido, you've had your fun
Professor Stupido, you are done!
Professor Stupido, your days of un-inventing are
  over
Because I un-invent you and I also un-invent
  the possibility of you ever un-inventing your
  un-invention ever again!'

'Ha!' said Professor Stupido. 'Your un-inventing rhyme doesn't even rhyme!'

'Doesn't matter,' said Terry as a bolt of un-inventing lightning leapt from his finger and zapped Professor Stupido right between the eyes.

Professor Stupido instantly disappeared.

'Well, that takes care of him,' said Terry, blowing on the tip of his finger to cool it down.

'I didn't know you had the power to un-invent things,' I said.

'Neither did I,' said Terry. 'But he just made me so angry. I guess un-inventing is not so hard after all.'

'But it *is* dangerous,' I said. 'Un-inventing something might solve one problem but it can cause a whole lot more. Promise me you'll never un-invent anything ever again.'

'I promise,' said Terry. 'I'll never ever, ever never un-invent anything ever EVER again . . . right after I un-invent that spider up there.'

'Uh-oh,' I said.

The End (or is it?)

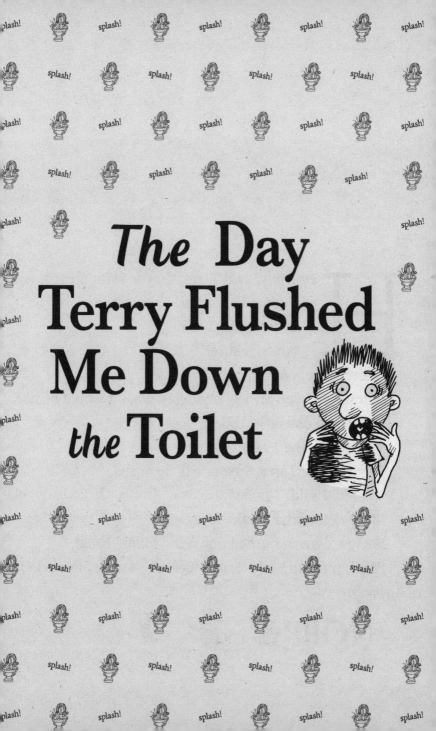

The Day Terry Flushed Me Down the Toilet

'**H**ey, Andy,' said Terry, 'do you want me to flush you down the toilet?'

'No thanks,' I said.

'Are you sure?'

'Pretty sure, yeah.'

'But haven't you always wondered what it would be like to be flushed down the toilet?'

'No, not really,' I said.

'Go on,' said Terry. 'Just one little flush.'

'I can't,' I said. 'I'm busy.'

'Busy doing what?' said Terry.

'Busy *not* being flushed down the toilet,' I said.

'Well, too bad,' said Terry. 'Because I'm going to do it anyway.'

'**NO!!!**' I shouted.

splash!

But it was too late.
The next thing I knew,
Terry had picked me up,
put me headfirst in the
toilet, and pushed the flush button.

After a long, watery ride,
I opened my eyes
to find myself at the
bottom of the ocean.
I could tell it was the
bottom of the ocean because
there was water everywhere,
a lot of sand and a whole
bunch of weird-looking fish.
Oh yeah, and a sign that said:

THE
BOTTOM OF
THE OCEAN.

I swam around looking for the exit until, in the distance, I
saw a magnificent sandcastle rising up from the sea floor.
It was decorated with seaweed, shells, sticks, bottle tops
and bits of broken glass and on the front door there was a
sign that said: **FREE AIR.**

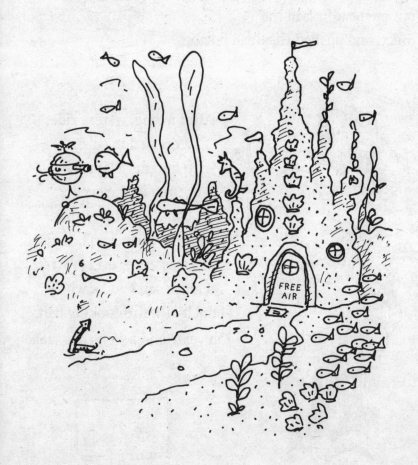

I'd been holding my breath ever since I was flushed, so the idea of *any* air—free or not—was very tempting. I swam through the door into an airlock, where there was no water—just air.

Cool, fresh, *free* air!

I took a deep breath.

And another.

And another.

I was just about to take another when I heard a

slithering

noise behind me.

I spun around to see a terrifying sea monster:

MERMAIDIA!

(If you're like most of our readers, you'll know that Mermaidia was a sea monster who pretended to be a mermaid and tricked Terry into marrying her and then tried to eat us both before we shrank her with our shrinking ray and flushed her down the toilet.)

'What are *you* doing here, Sandy?' said Mermaidia menacingly.

'My name's *Andy*, not *Sandy*,' I said. 'And I'm here because I got flushed down the toilet.'

'Welcome to the club,' said Mermaidia.

'What club?' I said.

'The flushed-down-the-toilet club,' said Mermaidia. 'It's not very nice, is it?'

'No,' I said.

'And *especially* not when I was a guest in your treehouse,' said Mermaidia.

'But you weren't *really* our guest,' I said. 'And you *were* threatening to eat us.'

'Well,' she said, waving her hand dismissively, 'it's all just water under the bridge or, more to the point, water down the S-bend—no hard feelings. I'm very happy to see you.'

'You are?' I said.

'Yes,' said Mermaidia. 'Because I'm very hungry, and now that I've caught you in my free-air trap, I know exactly what— or rather *who*—I'm having for dinner!'

'Not so fast!' said an even more familiar voice behind me.

I turned around. 'Terry?' I said. 'What are you doing here?'

'Well, I tried to get you out of the toilet with a plunger,' he said, 'but it didn't work. So I flushed myself down and came to see if you were okay.'

'Well, well, well!' said Mermaidia, licking her sea-monstery lips. 'If it isn't my long-lost husband. Better late than never, I suppose. I've already got my dinner, but you can be my **dessert!'**

'Not so fast!' said another familiar voice. This time we all turned around to see . . .

'Jill?' I said. 'What are you doing here?'

'I've come to rescue you and Terry,' she said.

'But how did you even know we were here?' said Terry.

'I didn't,' said Jill. 'I was just on a routine deep-sea surveillance mission looking for animals in trouble when I heard voices.'

'Ahem,' said Mermaidia. 'Do you mind? I'm just about to eat my dinner.'

'Actually, I *do* mind,' said Jill. 'Andy and Terry are my friends, and I'd really rather that you *don't* eat them.'

'Well, I'd really rather that I *do*,' said Mermaidia. 'And now that I think about it, you'll make a very tasty little after-dinner snack!'

'**Not so fast!**' said another voice. 'Nobody's going to be eating anybody—not if I have anything to do with it.'

We all turned to see Bill the postman!

'Bill?' I said. 'What are you doing here?'

'Just on my regular Pacific Ocean mail run,' said Bill. 'Fish send a lot more letters than people realise. The question is, what are *you* all doing here?'

'They came for dinner,' said Mermaidia. 'Well, when I say they came for dinner, I mean they came to *be* dinner.

Just like you.'

'I'm afraid not,' said Bill. 'I'm much too busy to stay for—or be—dinner. And besides, Andy, Terry and Jill are some of my favourite people in the whole world to deliver letters to. I'd miss them if you ate them.'

'All the more reason for me to eat you as well,' said Mermaidia. 'It means you'll be together forever and ever and ever!'

'Not so fast!' said a sweet voice.

We turned to see Mary Lollipoppins.

'Who are you?' said Mermaidia.

'I'm Mary Lollipoppins,' said Mary. 'The treehouse lollipop-serving robot. How about we all have an underwater lollipop party instead? That will be much more fun than eating a load of smelly people.'

'I'm not smelly!' said Terry.

'Shhh,' I whispered to Terry. 'She's on *our* side.'

'Hmmm . . .' said Mermaidia. 'I do *like* lollipops. They're my weakness—along with people, of course. Do you happen to have people-flavoured lollipops?'

'Of course!' said Mary, pulling out a handful of people-shaped lollipops. 'Here you go!'

Mermaidia snatched the lollipops out of Mary's hand. 'Let the great underwater lollipop party begin!' she said, then shoved them all into her mouth at the same time.

'Not so fast!' said a stern voice behind us.

Uh-oh. I already knew who it was, but I turned around to see anyway.

The Story Police!

'We're putting a stop to this story right now,' said the chief of the Story Police. 'It was already silly, but now it's downright illegal.'

'But we weren't doing anything wrong,' Mermaidia mumbled through her lollipops.

'Yes, you were,' said the chief, consulting his notebook. 'So far, the crimes of this story include:

- over-use of the word **"toilet"**
- the misuse of toilets in general
- four counts of attempted cannibalism
- the introduction of too many characters too quickly
- intention to hold an underwater lollipop party without a permit
- and over-use of the phrase **"not so fast"**.

snack
food

'You are all
under arrest . . .
forever!'

Quiet!

'Not so fast!' I said. 'There's no time to arrest anybody, because it's the end of the story.'

'That's the silliest and most unsatisfying end to any story ever,' said the chief. 'I've got a good mind to add that to the charge sheet!'

'No, you won't,' I said.

'Oh really?' said the chief. 'And why not?'

'I already told you,' I said. 'Because it's—

The End

The
Big Brain
Blockage

'Hey, Andy,' said Terry, 'I've got this really great idea for a story but I can't think of the words or pictures to explain it. I think my brain is blocked. Can you take a look?'

'Sure,' I said.

I shone a torch into Terry's right ear and peered deep inside his head.

large pea-size brain

↑ TERRY

'What can you see?' said Terry.

'Nothing,' I said.

'I'm not even sure you've got a brain! I can smell freshly baked cookies, though. Have you been been baking cookies in your ear by any chance?'

'No,' said Jill, appearing with a batch of freshly baked cookies. 'But *I* have.'

'You've been baking cookies in Terry's ear?' I said.

'No, in my oven,' said Jill. 'What's the matter with Terry?'

'His brain is blocked,' I said. 'He's got a great idea for a story but he can't get it out. I think we're going to have to operate.'

'Yay!' said Jill. 'I love operations. And as luck would have it, I just baked this batch of **shrink-me-down cookies**. If we eat a couple, we can make ourselves small enough to enter Terry's head and perform the operation right now.'

'Thanks, Jill,' said Terry, reaching for a cookie. 'Don't mind if I do!'

'And I don't mind if you *don't*!' I said, slapping his hand away from the cookies. 'You have to stay big while Jill and I get small— otherwise we won't be able to fit inside your head.'

'But I *like* cookies!' said Terry.

'Don't worry,' said Jill. 'Once we have your brain unblocked, you can eat all the cookies you want and get as small as you like. In the meantime, we need you to lie down and go to sleep so it's safe for us to conduct our intracranial investigation.'

'All right,' said Terry, and he lay down and closed his eyes.

'Are you asleep yet?' I said, after a few minutes.

'No,' said Terry. 'I need a glass of warm milk. I always have a glass of warm milk before I go to sleep.'

So I got him a glass of warm milk and he drank it all down—

 but he didn't fall asleep.

'I'm still awake,' said Terry.
'Can you sing me a lullaby?'

'I don't know any,' I said.

'Just a song, then,' said Terry.

'Which one?'

'How about my favourite song?' said Terry. 'The theme to The Barky the Barking Dog Show.'

'But that's the most boring song in the whole world,' I said.

'That's good,' whispered Jill. 'The more boring it is, the sooner he'll get to sleep and the sooner we can remove whatever's blocking his brain and the sooner he'll be able to tell you his story idea.'

Jill was right, of course, so I started to sing.

He barks all day
He barks all night
He barks and barks with all his might
His bark is much worse than his bite
He's Barky the Barking Dog

He barks at a cat
He barks at a shark
He barks in the street
He barks in the park
ALL he does is BARK BARK BARK
He's Barky the Barking Dog!

Barky barks up
Barky barks down
He's the barkingest barking dog in town
He's Barky the Barking Dog!

He barks at a hole
He barks at a tree
He barks at you
And he barks at me
He's Barky the Barking Dog!

'Okay, you can stop now,' said Jill, after I'd sung another few million verses. 'He's fast asleep. Quick, eat a cookie and we'll go in before he wakes up.'

We each ate a cookie and began to get smaller . . .

and smaller . . .

and smaller . . .

until we were each no bigger than

the size of the full stop at

the end of this

sentence.

We entered Terry's right ear and picked a path through a valley of boulders made of earwax until we came to a big pink crinkly thing.

'Hey, look!' I said, jumping up and down on it. 'Terry's got a trampoline in his brain!'

'I don't think it's a trampoline,' said Jill. 'I think this *is* Terry's brain. Be careful you don't fall into any of the cracks.'

'Oops, too late!' I said, falling into one of the cracks.

'Oops, too late for me, too,' said Jill, falling in after me.

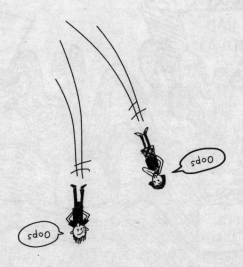

We landed in a stream. It wasn't
like an ordinary stream, though—
it was a stream of thought!
Or, more precisely, thoughts and ideas.

There was every type of

...idea you could think of!

'Hey, we can find out all of Terry's secrets!' I said.

'I don't think that's such a good idea,' said Jill. 'Secrets are secret. I think we should concentrate on clearing his brain blockage and then get out before we start to get big again.'

We floated slowly along and then the stream got so slow it was hardly even moving.

'There's definitely a blockage up ahead,' said Jill.

'Yeah, and it's getting really hot, too,' I said. 'If I didn't know better, I'd say a giant fire-breathing rubber duck is blocking our path!'

'A giant fire-breathing rubber duck *is* blocking our path,' said Jill. 'And it's not happy about us being here.'

The giant rubber duck directed a hot quack of fiery breath at us.

We ducked under the stream.

'I wish I'd brought my anti-fire-breathing rubber duck mirror,' I said.

'Don't worry,' said Jill. 'I've got mine.'

The duck quacked another deadly blast of flame at us.

I held my breath as Jill raised her mirror up and angled it towards the duck.

It worked! The flames bounced off the mirror and hit the duck. It let out an angry quack and then melted back into the stream.

'Great job, Jill!' I said. 'The stream is flowing really fast now. It's no longer blocked!'

'Let's go!' said Jill. 'We've already been in here longer than we should have.'

'Okay,' I said. 'But which way is the exit?'

'That way!' said Jill, pointing at a sign between two dark, hairy tunnels. 'Pull on these nostril hairs and, with a bit of luck, we might be able to make Terry sneeze. It might be a rough exit, but at least it will be fast.'

We each tugged on a hair and, before we knew it, Terry did the biggest sneeze ever and we shot out of his nose, back into the treehouse.

We started growing bigger,

and bigger,

and bigger,

until we were back to our regular size.

'Oh, hi,' said Terry sleepily. 'Did it work? Did you unblock my brain?'

'You tell us,' I said. 'Can you remember the story idea?'

'Yes!' said Terry. 'I *do* remember! It was an idea for a story about me having a blocked brain, which you and Jill fix by going inside my head and fighting a giant fire-breathing rubber duck!'

'That's the most ridiculous idea for a story I've ever heard!' said Jill.

'Oh,' said Terry, disappointed. 'So you don't like it?'

'Are you kidding?' said Jill.

'I love it! I'd really like to read that story.'

'And I'd really like to draw it!' said Terry.

'Great!' I said. 'Because I'd really like to *write* it!'

So I did.

The End

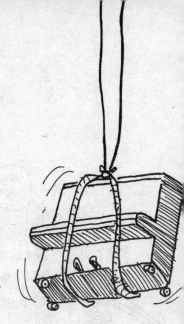

'Hey, Andy,' said Terry, 'can you stand under this piano?'

'What piano?' I said.

'That one up there,' he said, pointing to a piano that was hanging from a rope slung over a branch of our tree. He was holding the other end of the rope in his hand.

'Why do you want me to stand under it?' I said.

'I can't tell you,' said Terry.

'It's a surprise.'

'You're not going to let go of the rope and make the piano fall on me, are you?'

'No way,' said Terry. 'You're my best friend in the whole world. Why would I want to drop a piano on you?'

'I don't know why,' I said. 'But you have done some pretty strange stuff in the past—like that time you used my head as a bowling ball, remember?'

'That was just a joke,' said Terry.

111

'Not for me it wasn't,' I said. 'And what about the time you pushed me into the shark tank?'

'That was just a joke too,' said Terry.

'Not for me it wasn't!' I said. 'And what about the time you invented an Andy-exploder and you exploded me?'

'Another joke,' said Terry. 'And a pretty good one, too!'

'But I got exploded!' I said.

'I know,' said Terry, 'but that's not *my* fault. I didn't *make* you go into the Andy-exploder.'

'No, but you did say that if I went into the Andy-exploder I'd get a big surprise.'

spleen

'And you did,' said Terry. 'You were surprised that you exploded!'

'I sure was,' I said. 'But it wasn't a *nice* surprise. How would you like it if I invented a Terry-exploder and exploded you?'

'I'd love it!' said Terry. 'It would be hilarious. But it will never happen, because you don't know how to make Terry-exploders.'

'Yes, I do,' I said. 'In fact, I'm going to go and invent one right now!'

'Good luck!' said Terry. 'But first, can you *please* stand under the piano?'

'How do I know it's not another one of your little "jokes"?' I said. 'I just don't think it's a good idea.'

'I think it *is* a good idea,' said Terry. 'But don't take my word for it—why don't you ask Jill what she thinks?'

'Ask me what I think about what?' said Jill, who'd just climbed up onto our level.

'Terry wants me to stand under the piano he's hung from that branch, but I'm worried he might drop it on me. He says he won't, though. Do you think I should trust him?'

'No, I don't,' said Jill. 'He's dropped things on me before.'

'No, I haven't,' said Terry.

'Yes, you have,' said Jill. 'What about that elephant?!'

'What elephant?'

'The one you dropped on me!'

'Oh, *that* elephant,' said Terry. 'That was just a joke!'

'Well, yes, it *was* funny,' said Jill. 'But it took me a whole day to wriggle out from underneath it. And what about the time you told me and all my animals to stand under a mouse and then you dropped the mouse on us?'

'Another joke!' said Terry. 'And nobody got squashed.'

'Maybe not, but my horse Larry got scared because he has mouse-a-phobia. And the mouse ended up with a bruised tail.'

'How was I to know that Larry was scared of mice?' said Terry. 'Or that mouse tails bruised so easily? But this is different— I swear. This is a piano, and I *know* that Andy isn't scared of pianos. And I pinky-promise that I won't drop it on you, Andy. In fact, I pinky-pinky-promise. No, I pinky-pinky-pinky-promise. You can't get a pinkier promise than that.'

'Well, in that case I'll do it!' I said.

'I don't think that's such a good idea,' said Jill.

'I know,' I said. 'But he's my best friend and he has pinky-pinky-pinky-promised not to drop the piano on me. What could possibly go wrong?'

'He could drop the piano on you,' said Jill.

'But I won't,' said Terry. 'Go on, Andy. Stand under the piano. It's perfectly safe.'

'Okay,' I said, and I stepped under the piano.

Terry could have dropped it on me right then, but he was true to his word and the piano remained suspended in the air above me.

'See?' said Terry. 'I told you I had a surprise for you, and the surprise is that I *didn't* drop a piano on you!'

'You're a true friend,' I said. 'Thank you for not dropping the piano on me.'

'Actually, I've got another surprise for you,' said Terry.

'What is it?' I said.

'I changed my mind,' said Terry.

'About what?' I said.

'About dropping the piano on you,' said Terry. 'I think I'm going to do it after all.

'I knew it!' said Jill.

'RUN,
ANDY,
RUN!'

But before I could run, Terry let go of the rope and the piano came plummeting towards me.

I don't know if your best friend has ever dropped a piano on you, but if they have you probably know that pianos are very heavy and they hurt a lot . . . unless you're wearing a falling-piano-proof-suit, that is.

Which I was! An invisible one!!

The falling piano hit the shoulder of my invisible falling-piano-proof-suit and bounced off, then flew through the air and landed right on top of Terry with a loud crashing smashing plinkety-

plonkety

falling-

piano-y

sound . . .

KER-RASH-CRASH-PLINKETY-PLONKETY-SMASH!

'**Ouch,**' said Terry, rubbing his head as we lifted the piano off him. 'Falling pianos hurt!'

'Of course they do!' I said. 'That's why I was wearing my invisible falling-piano-proof-suit. You never know when your best friend might surprise you by dropping a piano on you.'

'Cool!' said Jill. 'Can I have a turn?'

'Sure,' I said.

'And can I have a turn after Jill?' said Terry.

'Of course!' I said.

And then we all took turns wearing the invisible falling-piano-proof-suit and dropping pianos on each other for the rest of the day.

Hit me, you stupid piano!

The End

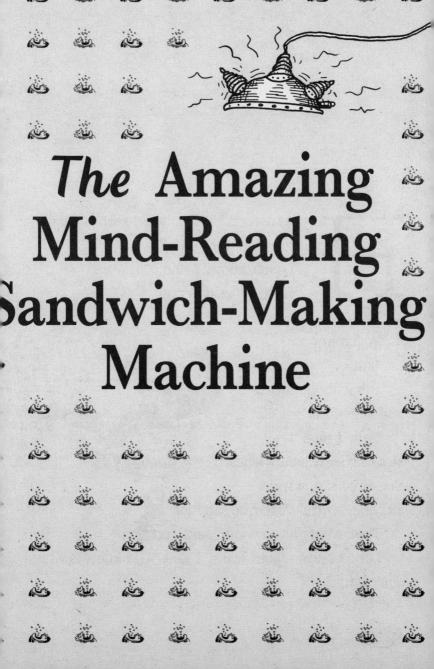

The Amazing Mind-Reading Sandwich-Making Machine

'H'ey, Andy,' said Terry, 'what sort of sandwich do you want for lunch?'

'I don't know,' I said.

'Cheese?' said Terry.

'Nah.'

'Vegemite?'

'Nah.'

'What about cheese *and* Vegemite?'

'Nah,' I said. 'I'm sick of cheese sandwiches, Vegemite sandwiches *and* cheese-and-Vegemite sandwiches.'

'Then what *do* you want?' said Terry.

'I don't know what I want,' I said. 'All I know is what I *don't* want!'

DING
DONG!

Terry looked over the edge of the deck. 'Bill the postman's at the front door!' he said.

'Hello, Andy and Terry!' called Bill. 'Special delivery for you.'

'Thanks, Bill,' I said. 'Can you just leave it at the door? We're kind of busy at the moment.'

'Making another silly book, I suppose,' said Bill.

'No,' I said. 'Just trying to decide what sort of sandwich to have for lunch.'

'Well, I think I may have something here that could help you,' said Bill.

'What is it?' said Terry.

'Judging by the label on the box,' said Bill, 'I'd say it's some sort of

<u>AMAZING</u> mind-reading
SANDWICH-MAKING MACHINE!

'That's exactly what we need!' I said. 'I ordered it last week. We'll be right down!'

It was quite a big box—so big that Bill had to help us carry it up to the kitchen. We took it out of the box and set it up.

'How does it work?' said Terry.

'It says in the instructions that it reads your mind to find out exactly what sort of sandwich you want and then it makes it for you!' I said. 'And even better, you can have your sandwich plain, lightly toasted, grilled or deep-fried. It will even blend the sandwich into a milkshake

so you can drink it, if that's what you really, *really* want!'

'Wow!' said Terry. 'Being able to drink a sandwich would save so much time! Let's get started.'

'Okay,' I said. 'Apparently, you just put this mind-reading helmet on and the machine does the rest. I'll go first.'

I put the helmet on and the machine whirred into life.

It buzzed
and flashed
and vibrated,
and then the strangest-looking toasted sandwich I'd ever seen came shooting out of the sandwich-dispensing chute.

'What sort did you get?' said Terry.

'I'm not sure yet,' I said, holding it up to my nose. 'It smells like chocolate.'

I took a bite. 'It *is* chocolate!' I said. I took another bite. 'And pizza . . . and marshmallows . . . and popcorn. It's all of them mixed together—all my favourite things in one perfectly toasted sandwich!'

'I'm going to try it now,' said Terry.

He put on the helmet and the machine hummed as it read his mind.

Pretty soon a very unusual-looking sandwich came shooting out. The bread was green with pink polka dots and the filling looked like rainbow-coloured fairy floss.

'What a funny-looking sandwich!' I said.

'It tastes funny, too,' said Terry, giggling. 'It's a *clown* sandwich! Who knew that's what I really, really wanted?'

'The AMAZING mind-reading

SANDWICH-MAKING MACHINE,'

I said. 'That's who!'

'I must admit, I'm feeling a little peckish myself,' said Bill. 'Mind if I have a turn?'

'Go right ahead!' said Terry.

Bill took his postman cap off and Terry helped him fit the helmet on.

Once again, the machine whirred into action—and out came a soggy-looking sort of sandwich.

It was dripping all over Bill's hands and running down his sleeves and face as he bit into it. But instead of being disappointed, Bill looked overjoyed.

'Mmmmmmmmm,' he said.

'An alphabet-soup sandwich! The machine must know

 how much I love letters!'

'I smell sandwiches!' said Edward Scooperhands, climbing
down the ladder onto our level.

'Yes,' said Terry. 'Our

AMAZING mind-reading

SANDWICH-MAKING MACHINE

is making them. Would you like one?'

'Well, yes,' said Edward, 'but I don't know what sort I want! I've never had a sandwich—I'm a robot, you know.'

'It doesn't matter,' I said. 'The

AMAZING mind-reading
SANDWICH-MAKING MACHINE

will read your mind and know exactly the sort of sandwich you need.'

We fitted the helmet and Edward closed his eyes.

The machine whirred and out came a sandwich covered in frost and ice.

'Ingenious!' said Edward as he bit into it.

'It's a nuts-and-bolts ice-cream sandwich! MAGNIFICENT!'

Word travelled fast around the treehouse, and soon there was a long line as everybody waited for a turn.

The _AMAZING_ mind-reading
SANDWICH-MAKING MACHINE

knew exactly what sort of sandwiches everyone wanted every time and produced almost every type of sandwich you could imagine . . . and plenty that I'll bet you couldn't.

There were fish-milkshake sandwiches for the penguins, peanuts-with-the-shell-on sandwiches for the Trunkinator, piping-hot lollipop sandwiches for Mary Lollipoppins, fancy three-decker sandwiches for Fancy Fish, fun-flavoured sandwiches for the circus folk, doorknob-cheesestick-poop-poop sandwiches for the three wise owls, pond-scum sandwiches for the baby dinosaurs,

tiny hay sandwiches for the tiny horses, man-flavoured sandwiches for the man-eating sharks, sawdust sandwiches for the rocking horses, stealth sandwiches with little black eye masks for the Ninja snails, straw sandwiches for the kind scarecrow, hobyah sandwiches for the dragon and sandwich-flavoured sandwiches for the sandwich-making machine (yes, even sandwich-making machines get hungry).

And so we all spent the rest of the afternoon eating sandwiches, until everybody was so full they couldn't eat a single sandwich more, no matter how perfect or delicious it was.

'If I eat another sandwich, I'm going to

explode!' I said.

I feel sick!

So do I.

'Me too,' said Jill. 'I wouldn't mind a pizza, though.'

'Great idea!' said Terry. 'Let's go to the make-your-own-pizza level and make one. What sort would you like?'

'I don't know,' said Jill. 'The trouble with the make-your-own-pizza level is that there are so many different toppings to choose from I can never decide what to have. I wish you had an

AMAZING mind-reading

PIZZA TOPPING-CHOOSING MACHINE

to choose them for us.'

DING DONG!

Terry looked over the edge of the deck. 'It's Bill again!' he said.

'Got another special delivery for you!' called Bill. 'Did any of you order an

AMAZING mind-reading

PIZZA TOPPING-CHOOSING MACHINE?'

'No,' I said. 'But Jill just *wished* for one!'

'Yay!' said Jill. 'It must have read my mind. We've had amazing sandwiches and now we're going to have perfectly topped pizzas—this is the **best day EVER!**'

The End

The Really Rainy Day

'Hey, Andy,' said Terry, 'how long has it been raining?'

'About three hours,' I said.

'Oh,' said Terry. 'How long now?'

'About three hours and five seconds,' I said.

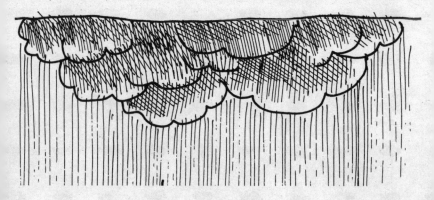

'And how long now?'

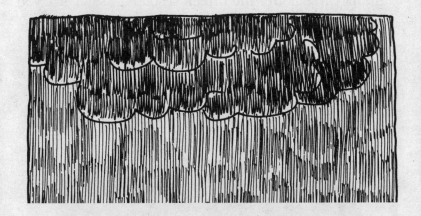

'About three hours and ten seconds,' I said.

'And now?'

'About three hours and fifteen seconds,' I said. 'Are you going to keep asking me how long it's been raining for the *entire* day?'

'No,' said Terry. 'Only until it stops raining. Which reminds me . . . how long has it been raining now?'

'About three thousand million billion years!' I shouted. 'Now stop asking me how long it's been raining. Let's do something else.'

'Like what?' said Terry.

'Let's play a game.'

'Yay!' said Terry. 'I love games. How about we play **LET'S PRETEND?'**

'Okay,' I said. 'What should we pretend?'

'You pretend to be a weather forecaster,' said Terry, 'and I'll ask you how long it's been raining and then you tell me.'

'**No,** that's a terrible idea,' I said. 'Besides, we've been playing that all morning anyway. Let's play **Snake Catcher!'**

'Only if *I* can be the snake catcher,' said Terry.

'No,' I said. 'That's my job. You have to be the snake.'

'But I was the snake last time,' said Terry.

'I know,' I said. 'And you were really good at it!'

'Then why did you hit me with a mallet?'

'Because you were going to bite me.'

'But I was a snake!' said Terry.
'That's what snakes are supposed to do,
isn't it? And you were supposed to
catch me, not *hit* me.'

'I *was* going to catch you,' I said.
'But how do you expect me to catch
you if I don't hit you first?'

'I don't know,' said Terry.

'That's why you can't be the snake catcher,'
I said. 'Because you don't know *anything*
about catching snakes.'

'How about we play **Shops** instead?'
said Terry. 'I'll be the shopkeeper
and you be a shopper.'

'Okay,' I said. 'Hello, is this a pet shop?'

'Yes,' said Terry. 'This is the **World's Greatest** pet shop in the world! What sort of pet would you like?'

'I'd like to buy a snake, please.'

'Certainly,' said Terry. 'Venomous or non-venomous?'

'Venomous, please.'

'One venomous snake coming up,' said Terry. 'Would you like that wrapped?'

'No thanks,' I said. 'I'll take it just as it is.'

'Here you go,' said Terry, pretending to hand me a snake.

So there was only one thing I could do—I pulled out a mallet and gave him a short, sharp tap on the head.

'**Ouch!**' he said. 'What did you do that for?'

'Because you were attacking me with a snake!'

'I wasn't attacking you!' said Terry. 'I was selling it to you. I'm a pet shop owner and this is a pet shop, right?'

'Yeah,' I said. 'But I'm still a snake catcher.'

'Not a very good one,' said Terry, rubbing his head. 'A proper snake catcher would be using a net, not a mallet.'

'Oh yeah,' I said. 'Good point. I need a net. Can this be a net shop and you be a net seller?'

'Sure,' said Terry. 'Good morning, sir, welcome to the **World's Greatest** net shop in the world! Would you like to buy a net?'

'Yes, please,' I said.

'Big, medium or small?' said Terry.

'Big,' I said. 'I'm a snake catcher, you see, and I need a net big enough to catch snakes of all sizes.'

'Certainly,' said Terry, handing me an imaginary net. 'Here you go. Would you like anything else?'

'Yes,' I said. 'I'd like to hit you with this mallet.'

'Sorry, sir,' said Terry. 'This is a net shop, not a hit-the-shopkeeper-with-a-mallet shop.'

'Oh, that's disappointing,' I said. 'Do you know where I can find a hit-the-shopkeeper-with-a-mallet shop?'

'Yes,' said Terry. 'Just one moment.'

Terry left the level and then came back wearing a suit made of bubble wrap. Every bit of him was covered from top to toe in bubbly plastic, even his head.

'Good morning, sir,' he said, through a small opening in the plastic. 'Welcome to the **World's Greatest** hit-the-shopkeeper-with-a-mallet shop in the world! How can I help you?'

'I'd like to hit you with a mallet, please,' I said.

'Hard, soft or medium?' said Terry.

'Pretty hard, I think,' I said.

'All right,' said Terry. 'When you're ready, you may hit me with a mallet.'

So I pulled out my mallet and whacked him as hard as I could.

'Didn't even hurt,' said Terry, producing his own mallet. 'Now it's my turn.'

'What do you mean?' I said. 'I'm the customer here.'

'Yes, and the rules of the hit-the-shopkeeper-with-a-mallet shop are that the customer and the shopkeeper take turns hitting each other with a mallet.'

'That's the dumbest rule I ever heard,' I said.

Terry just shrugged. 'I don't make the rules, sir. I just run the shop. Are you ready for me to hit *you* with a mallet?'

HIT-THE
SHOPKEEPER-
WITH-A-MALLET
SHOP RULES

The shopkeeper and customer take turns hitting each other with a mallet

One hit per turn

'Do I get a bubble wrap suit?' I said.

'No,' said Terry. 'You'd need to go to the bubble wrap suit shop for that.'

'Is there one around here?'

'Yes, but it's closed.'

'Can I borrow your suit?'

'I'm afraid not,' said Terry. 'I'm using it, and I never know when a new customer might come in. So,

get ready . . .'

'**Wait,**' I said. 'I've got a better idea. Let's play a different game.'

'What do you have in mind?'

'Well,' I said, 'let's pretend I'm Andy.'

'Okay,' said Terry. 'And who am I?'

'You can pretend to be Andy's friend Terry.'

'Cool,' said Terry. 'And where do we live?'

'In the **World's Greatest** treehouse in the world,' I said.

'Okay, I'm *definitely* interested,' said Terry. 'This sounds like fun. And what happens then?'

'Well, we're in the tree and it's raining outside and I ask you how long it's been raining.'

'Let's start right now!' said Terry.

'Sure,' I said. 'How long has it been raining?'

'About four hours,' said Terry.

'Oh,' I said. 'How long now?'

'About four hours and five seconds,' said Terry.

'And how long now?'

'About four hours and ten seconds,' said Terry.

'How long now?'

'About four hours and fifteen seconds,' said Terry. 'Are you going to keep asking me how long it's been raining for the entire day?'

'No,' I said. 'Just until you've forgotten about the mallet.'

'What mallet?' said Terry.

The End

The Wishing Well

'H ey, Terry,' I said. 'Did you borrow my pencil sharpener?'

'Yes,' said Terry.

'Can I have it back?'

'No,' said Terry.

'Why not?'

'Because I ate it.'

'You *ate* it?'

'Yeah,' said Terry. 'I was hungry. I wanted a banana cream pie but I couldn't find one, so I ate the pencil sharpener instead.'

'I wish you hadn't done that,' I said.

'So do I,' said Terry. 'It didn't taste very nice.'

'Of course it didn't!' I said. 'It was a pencil sharpener.'

'Do you know what *I* wish?' said Terry.

'No, what?'

'I wish we had a wishing well,' said Terry.

'We *do*,' I said. 'It's on the wishing-well level, remember?'

'Yay!' said Terry. 'I got my wish! I wish we could go there right now!'

'We can!' I said.

'Yay!' said Terry. 'I got another wish, and we're not even at the wishing well yet!'

I was about to explain to him that to get a true wish you have to make your wish and then throw a wishing-well coin down the wishing well, but at that moment Jill arrived.

'Hi, Jill!' said Terry. 'We're going to the wishing-well level. Do you want to come?'
'Ooh, yes, please,' said Jill.

So we began climbing.

On the way we stopped at Pinchy McPhee's Two-Dollar Shop and bought three wishing-well coins. And we got a real bargain, too— the coins are normally two dollars each but we got three for six dollars!

We continued climbing.

'All this climbing is making me even hungrier than I was before,' said Terry. 'I wish we were there already.'

'We are!' I said.

'Yay!' said Terry. 'I got *another* wish!'

We all stood around the wishing well.

'What are you going to wish for, Terry?' said Jill.

'I'm going to wish for a banana cream pie,' said Terry. 'No, *two* banana cream pies—no, hang on, I'm going to wish for

one thousand

banana cream pies!
What are you going
to wish for, Jill?'

m going to wish for a magical unicorn so I can go rainbow hunting!' said Jill.

'Magical unicorns always know where to find rainbows. What are you going to wish for, Andy?'

'I'm going to wish for a pencil sharpener,' I said.

'A pencil sharpener?' said Terry. 'But that's *boring*!'

'Ordinary pencil sharpeners, yes,' I said. 'But I'm not going to wish for an ordinary pencil sharpener. I'm going to wish for a pencil sharpener that can sharpen *any* pencil, no matter how **big** or how small.'

'I wish I'd thought of that!' said Terry. 'Never mind—too late now. Everybody get their coins ready.'

We held our wishing-well coins above the
wishing well, closed our eyes, made our
wishes and then dropped the coins
into
the
well.

The next thing we knew, I had a brand-new all-size pencil
sharpener in my hand and Jill was sitting on a magical
unicorn. There was also an enormous pile of banana
cream pies beside us. It was the most enormous pile of
pies I'd ever seen. Think of the biggest pile of pies you can
imagine, then double it—and double it again. *That's* how
big a pile it was.

'Help!'

shouted a muffled voice.

'That sounds like Terry,' I said. 'But I can't see him.'

'I think he's under all those pies,' said Jill.

'Help me!' said Terry.

'I'm being squashed by one thousand banana cream pies!'

'Don't worry,' I said. 'We'll have you out in no time! Quick, Jill, help me eat them!'

'But I don't like banana cream pies,' said Jill.

'What are you talking about?' I said. '*Everybody* likes banana cream pies.'

'Not me,' said Jill. 'They're too creamy and I don't like the taste of bananas.'

'What about the magical unicorn?' I said. 'Does it like banana cream pies?'

160

'No,' said Jill. 'Magical unicorns only eat fairy bread. But it could help by using its horn as a spike and flicking the pies into your mouth at high speed.'

'Perfect!' I said.

So that's what we did.

Jill's magical unicorn started stabbing the pies and flicking them into my mouth as fast as I could eat them.

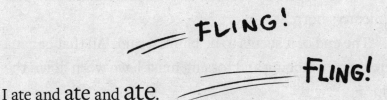

I ate and ate and ate.

And ate and ate and ate. FLICK!

And ate and ate and ate.

And ate and ate and ate…

until I'd eaten enough pies that Terry could sit up and help me eat the rest.

'Thanks, Andy,' said Terry when all the pies were eaten. 'And thanks to you, too, magical unicorn!'

'I'm not so sure how magical it is,' said Jill. 'I think there's something wrong with its horn. It's not glowing like it was before.'

We all crowded around and examined the magical unicorn's horn.

'The end of it seems to be blunt,' I said. 'All that banana cream pie stabbing and tossing must have worn down the tip.'

'Oh no,' said Jill. 'All of a unicorn's magical powers come from its horn. The sharper they are, the more magic power they hold.'

'Never fear,' I said. 'My all-size pencil sharpener is here!'

I sharpened the tip of the unicorn's horn until it was as sharp as the tip of a freshly sharpened pencil.

Before I'd even removed the pencil sharpener the horn started glowing again.

'You fixed it!' said Jill. 'Let's go for a ride! We can hunt for rainbows.'

'Do you think we'll find a banana cream pie at the end of a rainbow?' said Terry hopefully.

'Surely you can't still be hungry, Terry?' I said. 'Especially not after eating all those pies.'

'*You* ate most of them,' said Terry. 'And yes, I *am* still hungry. In fact, I just ate your new pencil sharpener.'

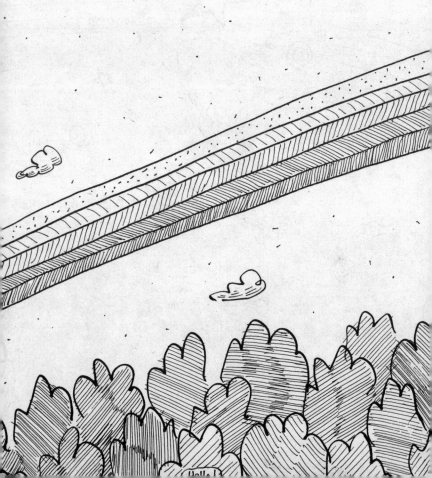

'Oh, great!' I said. 'Hey, Jill, can you find pots of all-size pencil sharpeners at the end of rainbows, too?'

'Normally it's pots of gold, but who knows *what* we'll find!' said Jill, and we all climbed on her new magical unicorn and flew off into the sky.

The End

The
Secret Secret

'Hey, Andy,' said Terry. 'Guess what?'

'What?' I said.

'I've got a secret.'

'What is it?'

'I can't tell you,' said Terry.

'Why not?'

'Because it's a secret,' said Terry.
'If I told you, then you'd tell
somebody else and then it wouldn't
be a secret any more.'

'I promise I won't tell *anybody*,'
I said. 'If you tell me I promise it
will *stay* secret for ever and ever.'

'Promise?' said Terry.

'Pinky-promise,' I said. 'With sugar on top.'

'Okay,' said Terry. 'Here goes.'

He leaned in close and whispered the secret in my ear.

'Wow,' I said. 'That's the most amazing secret I've ever heard!'

'Promise you won't tell anybody?' said Terry.

'Promise you won't tell anybody *what*?' said Jill, walking into the room.

'The amazing secret Terry just told me,' I said.

'What is it?' said Jill.

'I can't tell you,' I said. 'I promised Terry I wouldn't tell anyone.'

'It's a secret!' said Terry. 'A *secret* secret.'

'Is it about me?' said Jill.

'No,' I said.

'Then *tell* me, *please*!' said Jill.

'I love secrets.'

'But if we told you,' I said, 'you'd tell all your animals and they'd tell all the other animals and then it wouldn't be a secret any more.'

'I swear I won't tell any of my animals,' said Jill.

'Not even Silky?' I said.

'Not *even* Silky,' said Jill. 'Now please tell me the secret, before I *burst*!'

I looked at Terry.

Terry looked at me, and then he nodded.

I leaned in close to Jill's left ear and Terry leaned in close to her right ear and we whispered the secret together.

Jill's eyes grew wide.

'So *that's* the secret,' she said. 'That's a *good* one. Have you told the readers yet?'

'No,' I said. 'There's too many of them. If we told the readers, they'd tell other readers and those readers would tell other readers and soon everybody in the entire world would know the secret and then it wouldn't be a secret any more!'

'Uh-oh,' I said. 'Here they come.'

'Who?' said Jill.

'The readers!'

I said. **'Look.'**

'TELL US! TELL US! TELL US!'

the readers chanted as they streamed
through the forest and surrounded our tree.

'TELL US!

TELL US!

TELL US!'

'Tell you what?' said Terry, pretending he didn't know what they were chanting about.

'**THE SECRET!**' shouted the readers. '**TELL US THE SECRET . . . OR ELSE!**'

'Or else what?' I said.

There was silence for a moment, and then the readers shouted:

'**OR ELSE . . . WE'LL HUFF AND WE'LL PUFF AND WE'LL *BLOW* YOUR TREEHOUSE DOWN!**'

'You can't blow our treehouse down,' said Terry. 'It's too big and too strong.'

'OH YEAH?' said the readers. **'WELL, WATCH THIS!'**

And the readers began to

And the readers began to

And the readers  and

until . . .

Terry said, 'All right, all right, we give in—stop HUFFING and PUFFING and we'll tell you the secret!'

But it was too late.

All that huffing and puffing had been too much for the treehouse, and the tree! The tree fell over with a mighty crash and the treehouse tumbled down and bits of it went flying all over the forest.

'Now look what you've done!' said Terry.

'WE'RE *REALLY* SORRY,' said the readers. **'BUT YOU WOULDN'T TELL US THE SECRET.'**

'If we tell you the secret, will you help us put the tree back up and rebuild the treehouse?' I said.

'YES, OF COURSE!' said the readers.

'But, Andy,' whispered Terry. 'We can't tell them the secret because then it won't be a secret any more.'

'I know,' I whispered back. 'But if we don't tell them the secret then we won't have a treehouse any more. What I think we should do is tell them the secret so that they help us to rebuild the treehouse, and then afterwards we'll give them a drink of this secret-erasing potion that I mixed up in the underground laboratory this morning. After they drink it, they won't be able to remember the secret!'

'I hope you're right,' said Terry.

'I'm *always* right,' I said.

'Except when you're wrong,' said Jill.

'Give me one example of a time when I was wrong,' I said.

'What about the time you thought Mel Gibbon was a monkey,' said Jill, 'which he isn't because he's a gibbon, and gibbons aren't monkeys.'

'Gibbons, monkeys— *whatever*!' I said. 'We don't have time for this now. We have to rebuild the treehouse.'

We gathered the readers around and told a few of them the secret, and then they passed it on to some more and then those readers passed it on to others until, eventually, they had all heard it. This took a long time, but once everybody knew the secret they were happy. And then they helped us to get the tree back into position and rebuild the treehouse.

In fact, the readers did *such* a good job of putting it all back together that it was even better than it was before they blew it down!

**'WE'RE SORRY WE HUFFED
AND PUFFED AND *BLEW* YOUR TREEHOUSE DOWN,'**
said the readers.

'That's okay,' I said. 'Forgiven *and* forgotten. Now you must be very thirsty after all that treehouse rebuilding so here's a drink for you all.'

'Yay!' said the readers. They each drank a big cup of secret-erasing potion and went home happy, having completely forgotten the secret that they'd all come streaming through the forest to find out in the first place.

Unfortunately—or, fortunately, really—Jill and Terry and I were also very thirsty. So thirsty, in fact, that we forgot *not* to drink the secret-erasing potion and we ended up forgetting the secret, too, which is just as well, I guess, because now the secret will remain a secret forever and ever and ever.

The End

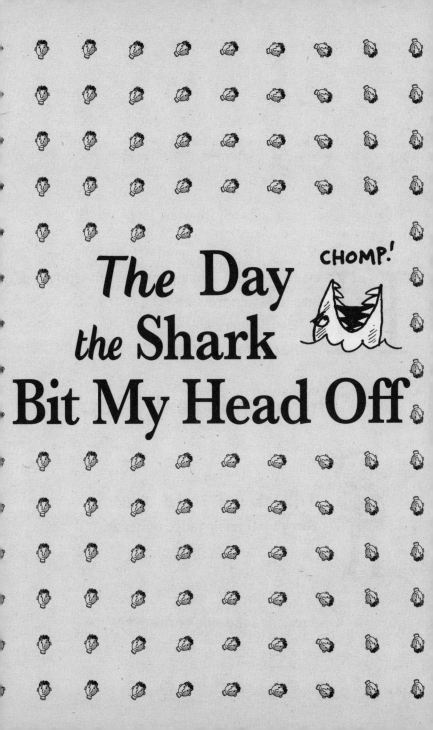

CHOMP!

The Day the Shark Bit My Head Off

'Hey, Andy,' said Terry, 'can you put this pizza into the oven for me?'

'Sure,' I said.

'Be careful,' said Terry.

'The oven is really hot.'

'I'll be the judge of that,' I said.
(Terry's a terrible judge of heat—
I'm *much* better.)

I touched the side of the oven.

'ARGHHHHHHH!'

I screamed as I pulled my finger away.

'That's really, really HOT!

Why didn't you tell me how hot it was?'

'I did,' said Terry. 'But you wouldn't listen.'

'Well, I would have if you'd told me it was *that* hot!' I said.

Just then Jill came into the pizza parlour. She was drinking a bottle of lemonade.

'What's going on?' she said. 'Why are you shouting at Terry?'

'Because he didn't warn me how hot the oven was and I touched it and burned my hand,' I said.

'I'm sorry to hear that,' said Jill. 'Would you like a sip of my lemonade to help take your mind off it? It's a really nice sherbet flavour.'

'Thanks,' I said, taking the bottle from Jill.

'Don't drink it too fast, though,' said Jill. 'It's extra fizzy!'

'I'll be the judge of that,' I said.
(Jill's a terrible judge of fizziness—
I'm *much* better.)

I took a big mouthful and a million billion tiny bubbles of fizziness almost burst my brain. (You've heard of brain freeze? Well this was brain FIZZ.)

'ARGHHHHHHH!'

I screamed as bubbles came out of my nose, my ears, my eyes and my mouth.

'That's really, really FIZZY!

Why didn't you warn me how fizzy it was?'

'I tried to,' said Jill. 'But you wouldn't listen.'

'I would have if you'd told me it was *that* fizzy,' I said.

Just then Edward Scooperhands came into the pizza parlour pushing a portable ice-cream cart.

'Get your extra-cold ice-creams, folks!' called Edward. 'Cold enough to give you brain freeze forever! You've been warned!'

I suppose you're probably thinking that I said, 'I'll be the judge of that,' and grabbed an extra-cold ice-cream, shoved it in my mouth and got brain freeze forever.

Well, I didn't.

I'm not stupid, you know.

Edward Scooperhands is a *very* good judge of the coldness of ice-cream! (Robots are much better judges of that sort of stuff than humans.)

'Oh, and by the way,' said Edward. 'On my way here I passed the tank full of man-eating sharks and the sharks seemed extra snappy. I don't think they've been fed. I gave them some ice-cream but I think it must have been too cold because they spat it out.'

'No problem, Edward,' I said. 'Thanks for letting me know. I'll go and feed them now.'

I grabbed a bucket of fish and headed to the tank. When I got there, the first thing I saw was a big sign that said: BE CAREFUL WHEN YOU'RE FEEDING THE SHARKS BECAUSE THEIR TEETH ARE SHARP ENOUGH TO BITE YOUR HEAD OFF.

 'I'll be the judge of that,' I said. (I'm a *much* better judge of shark-tooth-sharpness than whoever wrote that sign and I really don't think the sharks' teeth are sharp enough to bite anybody's head off.)

I stood close to the edge of the water and the sharks rushed towards me.

Edward was right. They *were* hungry! They were leaping out of the water, biting the fish right out of my hands and then, in the frenzy, one jumped up extra high and *bit my head off*!

'ARGHHHHHHH!'

I screamed—or, rather, my head screamed.

'A SHARK BIT MY HEAD OFF!'

But nobody heard me.

Fortunately the sharks were full of fish by this time and seemed more interested in using my head as a volleyball than eating it.

They were merrily snout-butting my head from one to the other until one of them butted my head a little too hard and it went flying out of the shark tank, and fell

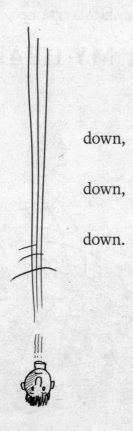

down,

down,

down.

It fell until it hit the trampoline and then it bounced

up,

up,

up.

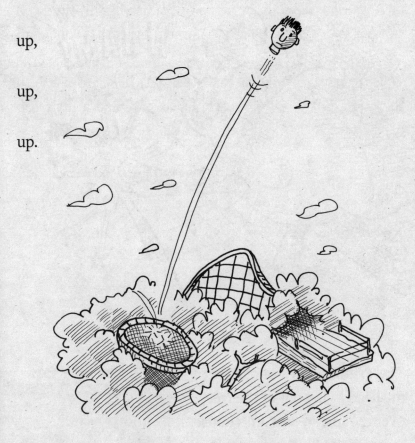

'Catch me!' I shouted at Terry and Jill as I passed them, but I was going too fast—they didn't even *see* me.

My head hurtled past them and flew up towards the Trunkinator's level, and when he saw my head he coiled his trunk into a tight spring and let fly.

The Trunkinator's punch sent
my head flying out of the tree,
over the forest, past Jill's house,
towards the Big Nose Books
building in the city.

My head smashed through
the window of Mr Big Nose's
office and bounced all around
the room.

'What is the meaning of this?' Mr Big Nose spluttered angrily. 'You have a book to write and it's due at five o'clock!'

'What time is it now?' I said.

'Three o'clock!' he said. 'You have two hours to deliver the manuscript to me . . . or else I'll be even angrier than I already am!'

'Um,' I said, 'that might be a problem. You see, my head's come off . . .'

'Yes, I can see that!' said Mr Big Nose. 'And I can see that it might be a problem, but it's *your* problem, not mine.'

'I understand, Mr Big Nose,' I said. 'Could you please put my head into that head cannon and fire it back into the treehouse, and I'll see what I can do.'

'All right,' said Mr Big Nose, pushing my head into the cannon and lighting the fuse, 'but remember, you've got TWO HOURS ...

or else!'

The cannon exploded with a bang and my head went flying back out the window, over the city, over the forest, past Jill's house, back into the tree and right down onto the neck of my body, which was still standing beside the shark tank where I'd left it.

I ran back to the pizza parlour, where Jill and Terry were still making pizzas.

'What took you so long?' said Terry.

'A shark bit my head off,' I said.

'It bit your head off?!' said Jill. '*Right* off?'

'Yes!' I said. '*Completely* off—and then the Trunkinator punched it so hard it flew across the forest right into Mr Big Nose's office.'

'Oh no!' said Jill. 'Was Mr Big Nose angry?'

'No angrier than usual,' I said. 'But he will be if we don't get our next book in on time—it's due at five o'clock today and we haven't even started it!'

'I've got an idea,' said Terry. 'Why don't we write a book about all the silly things that have happened in the treehouse that we haven't written about in our other books?'

'But most of those stories are too silly to be told,' I said.

'Until now, yes,' said Terry. 'But this is an emergency. We could call it, *Treehouse Tales Too Silly to Be Told—Until Now*!'

'That's a silly idea,' I said. 'So silly it might just work!'

'Let's do it!' said Terry.

So we did. And then Jill flew us to Mr Big Nose's office in her flying cat sleigh and we delivered the book at exactly five o'clock.

'Phew,' I said, when we were back in the pizza parlour, 'I'm glad that's over.'

'Me too,' said Terry. 'Would you like a slice of chilli pizza?'

'Yes, please,' I said.

'Careful,' said Jill. 'The chillies are extra hot.'

'I'll be the judge of that,' I said.

The End

Lots of laughs

at every level!

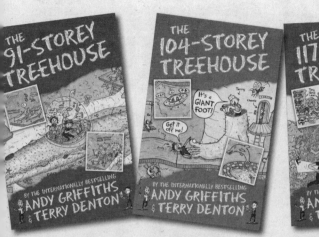

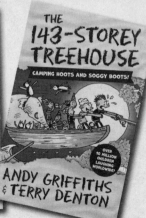

Lots of laughs

at every level!

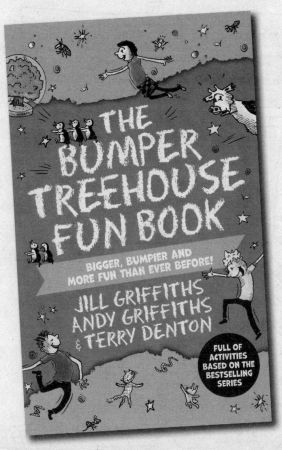